The Merry Christmas Book

A first book of holiday stories and poems

ILLUSTRATED BY
DENISE FLEMING

Random House 🏠 New York

For David, still the one.
—D. F.

The publisher wishes to thank the following for permission to reprint:

William Morrow & Company for *A Christmas Fantasy* by Carolyn Haywood. Copyright © 1972 by Carolyn Haywood. By permission of William Morrow & Company. Aileen Fisher for "Country Christmas." By permission of the author. Plays, Inc., Publishers, Boston, MA, for "Christmas Shoppers" by Aileen Fisher. Reprinted by permission from YEAR-ROUND PROGRAMS FOR YOUNG PLAYERS by Aileen Fisher. Copyright © 1985 by Aileen Fisher. Marchette Chute for "Christmas" from AROUND AND ABOUT by Marchette Chute. Copyright © 1957 (E. P. Dutton), renewed 1985 by Marchette Chute. Reprinted by permission of the author. Bobbi Katz for "A Christmas Card for Santa." Copyright © 1981 by Bobbi Katz. Used by permission of the author. Alfred A. Knopf, Inc., for *One Thousand Christmas Beards* by Roger Duvoisin. Copyright © 1955 by Roger Duvoisin. Reprinted by permission of Alfred A. Knopf, Inc. William Morrow & Company for "Our Christmas Play" from IT'S CHRISTMAS by Jack Prelutsky. Copyright © 1981 by Jack Prelutsky. By permission of Greenwillow Books (A Division of William Morrow & Company).

The Nutcracker and *The Fir Tree* from MY LITTLE LIBRARY OF CHRISTMAS CLASSICS. Text copyright © 1983 by Random House, Inc. *The Christmas Story Based on the Gospels According to Saint Matthew and Saint Luke,* retold by Deborah Hautzig, copyright © 1981 by Random House, Inc.

Library of Congress Cataloging-in-Publication Data:

Fleming, Denise. The merry Christmas book. SUMMARY: A collection of poems and stories, including "The Nutcracker," Andersen's "Fir Tree," and "The Night Before Christmas," especially intended for preschoolers. 1. Christmas—Literary collections. [1. Christmas—Literary collections] I. Title. PZ5.F6Me 1986 808.8′033 86-3258 ISBN: 0-394-87955-4 (trade); 0-394-97955-9 (lib. bdg.)

Manufactured in the United States of America 1 2 3 4 5 6 7 8 9 0

CONTENTS

THE CHRISTMAS STORY

BASED ON THE GOSPELS ACCORDING TO SAINT MATTHEW AND SAINT LUKE

retold by Deborah Hautzig

Long ago in the city of Nazareth there lived a carpenter named Joseph and his wife, Mary. They had a small house, and they had a donkey, but they did not have any children.

One day when Mary was alone in the garden, an angel appeared. It was the angel Gabriel. Mary did not know why Gabriel had come, and she was afraid.

"Do not be afraid, Mary," the angel said. "You are special and favored by God, and He has chosen you to be the mother of his son. Your son's name will be Jesus. He will be born a king and his kingdom will never end."

Mary was very happy.

When it was almost time for Mary to have her baby, Joseph said, "We must take a trip to Bethlehem to pay our taxes. It is a long journey, but you can ride our donkey." And so they went.

When Mary and Joseph came to Bethlehem, it was late at night and they were very tired. But there was no room for them at the inn. The innkeeper said they could sleep in the stable, so they went there to rest for the night.

In the stable were a cow, a lamb, a goat, and a dove. The animals were friendly. They let Joseph and Mary use their hay for a bed.

That very night Mary's child was born. She wrapped him in soft cloth to keep him warm. There was no crib for the baby, so Mary laid him in the animals' manger.

In the fields outside of Bethlehem, shepherds watched over their flocks of sheep. Suddenly a light appeared in the night sky. The shepherds looked up and saw an angel. They were afraid until the angel spoke.

"I am bringing you news of great joy," said the angel. "Tonight in the city of Bethlehem, a savior has been born. He is called Jesus Christ, and he is our Lord. You will find the baby wrapped in swaddling clothes, lying in a manger."

The shepherds went to Bethlehem. When they found the stable, they were filled with joy at the sight of the child and knelt beside the manger to honor him. Then they went out to tell people what the angel had said about the newborn baby.

Far away in the East lived three wise men named Caspar, Melchior, and Balthazar, who had watched the skies for many years. They knew that someday a new star would rise to announce the birth of their king.

At last it appeared—a bright, glowing star they had never seen before.

The wise men set out to follow the star. They traveled westward across many miles of desert. The star was their guide. It led them to Bethlehem. Then it came to rest right above a little stable.

The wise men entered the stable, and when they saw the baby they knew they had found their king. They gave him gifts of gold and wonderfully scented perfumes, frankincense and myrrh.

The wise men worshiped the child as the shepherds had, and they rejoiced.

Even the animals in the stable knew how special this baby was. Everyone knew he would be kind and gentle. They knew he would be a wise teacher, and a friend to all animals and to all people.

And he was. Every year at Christmas time we celebrate the birth of Jesus Christ, because he brought the good news of God's love to all living things.

A CHRISTMAS FANTASY

by Carolyn Haywood

nce there was a little boy whose name was Claus. He had a round merry face with cheeks like rosy apples, a perfect cherry of a nose, and bright blue eyes that seemed to dance in his head. When he laughed he bounced like a rubber ball and shouted, "Ho! Ho! Ho!" So everyone else laughed too. He lived with his godmother in a beautiful little house with gingerbread trim.

Now Claus's godmother never knew where he came from. She found him, one Christmas morning, when he was a tiny baby, lying on the hearth. He was rattling his belt of sleigh bells and kicking his little fat feet, which were covered with bright red socks. How he got there, his godmother had no idea.

She became more and more certain, though, as he grew older, that he had been dropped down the chimney, for Claus never could remember to come into the house through the door. He even wouldn't come in through the window, but always came tumbling down the chimney. When his godmother asked him why he always came in by the chimney, he said, "Because I never need a latchkey, and it never bangs," which of course was a very good reason. So by the time Claus was four years old, everyone was used to having him drop down the chimney for a call.

He was such a jolly little fellow that everyone loved him. His godmother dressed him in a bright red suit to match his red socks, and he always wore his sleigh-bell belt. As he grew bigger his belt grew longer, and each year a new bell appeared.

His red socks were always just the right size for his feet and they never wore out, which was very nice for his godmother, because she never had to do any darning.

Now Claus's godmother loved him so much she decided to give him a present every day. So every night, after Claus was sound asleep, his godmother tiptoed into his room and put a present in one of his red socks. No matter how big the present was it always fit in the sock, and no matter how tiny it was it always filled the sock. Every morning, when Claus woke up, he reached for his sock and pulled out his present. Then he jumped up and down, laughed merrily, and shouted, "Ho! Ho! Ho! What a wonderful present! It's just what I wanted." By the time Claus was six years old, the whole house was so full of presents that his godmother had to move into the house next door.

Now, when Claus was six years old, he started to go to school, and because he was such a jolly little fellow, all of the boys and girls loved him. Every morning the children marched into school and took their seats. Then there was a patter on the roof, a tinkle of bells, and down the chimney came Claus.

"Claus," the teacher said, "why don't you come in the door with the other children?"

Claus laughed his merry laugh and said, "I never can remember until I'm halfway down the chimney, and then it's too late to go back."

One of the first things that Claus learned when he went to school was that other children did not have presents in their socks every morning, and this made him very sad. "I know," he said to himself, "I'll give all the good children the presents that fill our house."

So he said to the boys and girls, "Whatever you want for a present, just let me know and I'll give it to you. But only if you've been good." The children were delighted, and so they began to write letters to Claus.

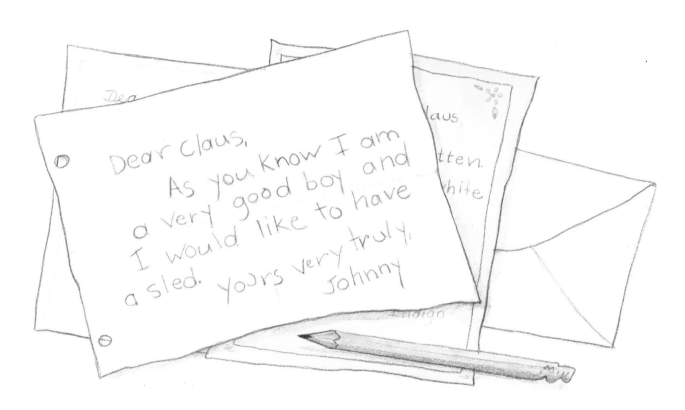

Claus would put the letter in his pocket, and then one night, after Johnny was sound asleep, Claus would drop down the little boy's chimney and leave a sled by his bed. Soon everyone called Claus "Good Claus."

One day his godmother said to him, "Claus, what do you want to be when you grow up?"

"Oh," replied Claus, "I want to be in the present business and give presents to all the children all over the world."

"But you can't run all over the world with presents!" said his godmother.

"I can do it once a year," replied Claus, "on Christmas eve."

And so, when little Claus grew up and had a long white beard, his godmother bought him eight reindeer and a beautiful sleigh, and every Christmas eve he piled his sleigh high with presents and dashed all over the world, dropping down chimneys and leaving toys in good little children's stockings.

And because he was never cross, but always loving and kind, he lives forever and all the boys and girls love him. They call him SANTA CLAUS.

COUNTRY CHRISTMAS
by *Aileen Fisher*

Let's hang up some suet
for juncos and jays,
let's put out some hay for the deer,
let's throw in some corn
where the cottontail stays,
this holiday season of year.

Let's scatter some millet
and barley and wheat—
it isn't much trouble or fuss
to give all the wild folk
a holiday treat
so they can have Christmas, like us!

JINGLE BELLS
by *James Pierpont*

Dashing through the snow,
In a one-horse open sleigh,
O'er the fields we go,
Laughing all the way;
Bells on bob-tail ring,
Making spirits bright;
What fun it is to ride and sing
A sleighing song tonight.

Jingle bells, jingle bells,
Jingle all the way;
Oh, what fun it is to ride
In a one-horse open sleigh.
Jingle bells, jingle bells,
Jingle all the way.
Oh, what fun it is to ride
In a one-horse open sleigh.

THE NUTCRACKER
THE STORY BASED ON THE BALLET

It was Christmas Eve and Marie and her brother, Fritz, could hardly wait for the party to start. At last the guests arrived. The drawing-room doors were flung open and a brilliance of light and color flooded the hall.

"Oh! It's the most beautiful Christmas tree in the world!" cried the children.

Hundreds of tiny candles twinkled like stars, and all sorts of sparkling ornaments and delicious things to eat hung from the branches. Under the tree were so many presents that the children didn't know what to look at first!

Godpapa Drosselmeir brought out his special gifts. He opened a tremendous box and out stepped a life-size toy soldier! Drosselmeir wound it up, and everyone watched in awe as it marched and danced around the room.

Then Drosselmeir got out from under the tree his gift for Marie and gave it to her. It was a wooden nutcracker shaped like a little man, with a white cotton beard and a cheerful smile from ear to ear. Though it was a small gift, it was the one Marie loved best of all.

Fritz called the nutcracker an ugly fellow and crammed the largest walnut into the poor nutcracker's mouth. Crack, crack—three teeth fell out.

"Stop it, Fritz! You're hurting him!" cried Marie as she snatched the nutcracker from her brother and cradled him in her arms.

"Keep your broken nutcracker," snorted Fritz. "What's the good of a nutcracker who can't do his job?"

Drosselmeir gave Marie his handkerchief, and she gently tied it around the nutcracker's jaw. Marie vowed to protect the little wooden man forever. She put him safely away in the toy closet.

Late that night, after the party was over and everyone was in bed, Marie crept quietly downstairs to the drawing room. The grandfather clock struck midnight. Marie stared at the chiming clock when suddenly Godpapa Drosselmeir appeared sitting at the top!

"Godfather! What a fright you've given me!" cried Marie. But before she could say another word, the most amazing thing happened.

The tree began to grow bigger and bigger, and the windows and toys and everything in the room grew with it. Now Marie seemed no bigger than a toy the size of the nutcracker!

Just then Marie was surrounded by an army of mice. Led by the monstrous seven-headed king of mice, they drew their swords and marched right up to the toy closet to challenge their enemy.

Drums beat, trumpets blared! It was the toys' call to arms. Soldiers, puppets, dolls, and even candy people rushed out. Then out of the closet leaped the nutcracker, flourishing his sword and leading the toys to battle.

Rank after rank of mice appeared. Marie watched in horror as the nutcracker's small army was driven back. At last three mice seized the nutcracker's sword.

"Now I have you!" squeaked the king of mice.

Marie could stand it no longer. "Oh, my poor nutcracker!" she cried. Then she threw her left shoe as hard as she could, directly at the king of mice. Instantly the mice disappeared as if by magic.

Marie turned to look at the nutcracker she loved so dearly, and before her eyes the homely nutcracker was transformed into a handsome young prince.

"My dearest lady," he said, kneeling before Marie, "you have saved my life. Now let me take you to my kingdom—the Land of Sweets."

Taking her by the hand, he led Marie out the window and into Christmas Wood. The snowflakes tasted like sugar; exquisite little snow fairies danced all around them, beckoning them on.

Marie and the little prince were greeted at his palace by a beautiful lady dressed in gossamer pink and white, who shimmered like a dewdrop.

"She is the Sugar Plum Fairy," said the little prince. He told the Sugar Plum Fairy of his battle with the king of mice and how Marie had saved his life.

The Sugar Plum Fairy gently kissed Marie. Then she clapped her hands, and little angels with golden wings and halos took their places for the fairies' dance honoring the homecoming of the little prince.

"And now," said the nutcracker prince, "to the banquet!" He led Marie through the dazzling marzipan palace into a crystal hall, and together they sat upon a golden throne.

Rich coffee from Arabia was brought by a veiled lady wearing tinkling bracelets; hot chocolate from Spain was brought by ladies in chocolate dresses.

Then Marie and the prince watched in delight as all of his loyal subjects appeared. Each brought something delicious to eat, and one by one they performed a dance.

Chinese dancers jumped out of a teapot and did a lively dance.

From Russia came the Dance of the Candy Canes.

From France came Mother Ginger and her little puppets, called Polichinelles.

The Waltz of the Flowers was led by the Sugar Plum Fairy.

Marie watched the splendor of the dances as though it were all part of a wonderful dream. "Everything and everyone here is so lovable and full of life," she said. "If only I could stay here forever!"

At last Marie and her nutcracker prince stepped into the
royal sleigh drawn by reindeer, and all the loyal subjects stood
by to bid them farewell. Marie and the prince waved as the
sleigh rose slowly into the glittering sky. Everyone in the Land
of Sweets waved back till the sleigh disappeared from sight.

CHRISTMAS SHOPPERS
by Aileen Fisher

Oh, the wind is brisk and biting
and the cold is not inviting,
but there's music, merry music everywhere.
The streets are full of bustle,
and our feet are full of hustle,
for there's Christmas, merry Christmas in the air.

Oh, the wind is cold and chilly
and it whistles at us shrilly,
but there's music, merry music everywhere.
The bells are full of ringing
and our hearts are full of singing,
for there's Christmas, merry Christmas in the air.

CHRISTMAS
by Marchette Chute

My goodness, my goodness,
It's Christmas again.
The bells are all ringing.
I do not know when
I've been so excited.
The tree is all fixed,
The candles are lighted,
The pudding is mixed.

The wreath's on the door
And the carols are sung,
The presents are wrapped
And the holly is hung.
The turkey is sitting
All safe in its pan,
And I am behaving
As calm as I can.

24

DO NOT OPEN UNTIL CHRISTMAS

by *James S. Tippett*

I shake-shake,
Shake-shake,
Shake the package well.

But what there is
Inside of it,
Shaking will not tell.

A CHRISTMAS CARD FOR SANTA

by *Bobbi Katz*

We all hung up our stockings,
and we left you a nice snack.
By now, I guess, dear Santa,
you have filled your heavy pack.
Your reindeer must be ready
to take you for a ride.
Do you have both your mittens?
It's so very cold outside.
Be careful, please, dear Santa,
on the rooftops where you go.
They're slanty and they're slippery
with a crust of ice and snow.

I guess I should be tired,
but I cannot fall asleep.
Tonight I'll count some reindeer,
instead of counting sheep.
I think you are the nicest man
to do the things you do.
Merry Christmas, Santa dear,
and a happy New Year, too!

ONE THOUSAND CHRISTMAS BEARDS

by Roger Duvoisin

At Christmas time, when snowflakes fly all about, when windows are hung with Christmas wreaths, and fir trees are bright with lights, all the Santa Clauses come out into the streets.

All the Santa Clauses? Are there many Santas? Or is there only one?

If you wish to know, open the door of Santa's igloo (only a little, not enough to let the cold come in), and listen:

"Am I angry!" Santa was saying to Mrs. Santa. "One hundred, one thousand times angry to see, when Christmas comes, so many people with red suits like mine, and false beards and wigs that make them resemble me.

"Wherever I go, I meet Santas—Santa Clauses everywhere! Some are fat and some are thin, some are tall and some are small, some have red noses like circus clowns, some are shabby and some are neat. By my own real beard, I'll put an end to those false Santas! There is only *one* Santa Claus, and *that's me!*"

"Do not excite yourself," said Mrs. Santa. "You will get hot and then catch cold. Soon you will forget all about it."

It was true that Santa could not be angry very long. The next day he worked at his toys as gaily and happily as ever.

But the following Christmas, when he went on his rounds and saw Santas all about town, he got angry all over again. With his face as red as his suit, he declared war on the false Santas. He hunted them in the streets—in the stores—in the subways. Wherever he found them, he sprang upon them and snatched their false beards away.

There was the doorman Santa, who helped people out of taxi cabs; he was a Santa as big as a bear with a pillow for a stomach. Santa snatched his beard and wig with a jerk and put them into his bag.

There was the sandwich man Santa, who was so thin his red suit hung on him like a flag on a pole on a windless day. Santa got his beard with a shout of victory.

There was the farmer Santa, who sold Christmas trees and beat his feet on the sidewalk to keep warm. He had a false red nose above his false beard. They were both put away into Santa's bag.

There was the trumpeter Santa, who stood at the curb and played on his trumpet. He played a screeching false note when Santa took his beard away.

There was the merchant Santa, who carried dolls on a tray and cried along the street: "Dolls for sale! A quarter for a doll!" The doll in his hand said "Mama!" when Santa pulled off this Santa's beard.

There was the shabby Santa, who had finished his day's work and waited for the subway to take him home.

There was also the Santa who sang "Silent Night" by a false chimney and sounded a bell to call passersby to drop their coins.

There was the wax Santa, who smiled day and night amidst the hats of the hat store window.

And the salesman Santa, who sat in a store to draw customers to his display of Christmas cards.

There was the tired Santa, who sat in a cafeteria with his cup of hot coffee. This one did not wait for Santa to snatch his beard. "Here, take it," he said. "I can't drink my coffee with it on."

There were more, many more false Santas! When Santa had pulled all their false beards and frightened them all into hiding, he was ready to ride back home.

Great was Santa's pride when he called Mrs. Santa out to show her his trophies: a sleighful of Christmas beards!

Alas, his pride melted away like a snowman in the sun when she looked at him and said severely, "Santa, you cruel man, did you kill all the false Santas who wore those false beards?"

"No, I didn't," said Santa, "but I put an end to their trying to look like me."

"Santa, you are so silly! You never stopped to think, did you, why there are lots of Santas about when Christmas comes. In how many places can you be at one time?"

"Why, *one,* of course."

"Then, how do you think people can have true Christmas cheer in their towns when they see you for only a moment or not at all?"

"They can't very well, can they?"

"Yes, they can. That's why so many dress like you; it makes the streets and the stores more cheerful. Children like to look at you so much! They would have a sad Christmas indeed with no Santa about."

Good Santa was now very sorry about all those beards in his sleigh. He wrapped them up into as many packages and mailed them all back to their owners. He even included a box of candy with each beard.

Thereafter, the more Santas he saw at Christmas time, the happier he was!

OUR CHRISTMAS PLAY

by Jack Prelutsky

We were nervous and excited
in assembly today,
for our parents came to visit us
and watch our Christmas play.
Our teachers helped a little,
but we did the most ourselves,
the fattest kid played Santa
and the smallest kids were elves.

A few were Santa's reindeer
so they got to run and leap,
some of us were shepherds,
and a bunch were woolly sheep,
there was Jesus in the manger,
there were angels wearing wings,
there was Joseph, there was Mary,
and the three wise Eastern kings.

We wore makeup, we wore costumes,
it was really lots of fun,
and our parents all applauded
when our Christmas play was done,
then we took our bows together,
everyone that is, but me—
I just stood there, green and fragrant,
for I played the Christmas tree.

THE FIR TREE

BASED ON THE FAIRY TALE
by Hans Christian Andersen

ut in the forest stood a pretty little fir tree. It had plenty of sunlight and fresh air, and all around grew many larger trees of all kinds. But the little fir tree was not happy. It took no pleasure in the sunshine and fresh air. It took no notice of the peasant children who came to look for strawberries. They would sit by the little fir tree and say, "How pretty and small this tree is!" The fir tree did not like to hear that at all! It only wanted to be great and big.

When it was winter and the snow lay sparkling all around, a hare would often come along and jump right over the little fir tree. This made the fir tree so angry!

"Rejoice in your youth," said the sunbeams. "Rejoice in your fresh growth and young life!"

But the fir tree did not understand. "Oh, if only I were as big as the others!" it said with a sigh. "Then I would spread my branches far around, and birds would build nests in my boughs, and I would nod grandly in the wind!"

Two winters went by, and when the third came, the tree had grown so tall that the hare had to run around it.

"Oh! To grow and grow and become old—it's the finest thing in the world!" the tree thought happily.

When Christmas time was near, many young trees were cut down and taken away on wagons. But not the fir tree.

"Where are they all going?" asked the fir tree. "Where are they being taken?"

"We know!" chirped the sparrows. "We looked in the town windows. We know where they go!

"They are put into warm rooms and dressed up in the most beautiful splendor," said the sparrows. "Gilt apples, honey cakes, toys, and hundreds of candles. They are called Christmas trees."

"Oh! How I long to be a Christmas tree!" cried the fir tree. "It is my greatest wish."

All year long the fir tree grew, and when Christmas came again, its wish came true. It was the first tree to be cut down. The axe cut deep, and the tree fell to the ground with a great sigh.

"I thought I would feel happy to leave," thought the tree. "But it is sad to leave my friends and my home."

The fir tree was no sooner taken to a yard when a man came and said, "This tree is perfect!"

So the fir tree was taken to a large house and put into a tub filled with sand. Then the servants and young ladies hung golden apples and walnuts from the branches. Dolls and toy soldiers swung on satin ribbons, and more than a hundred colored candles were fastened to different boughs. On the top was fixed a glittering gold star.

"This evening," said the young ladies, "this tree will shine and shine!"

The tree could hardly wait for evening to come!

At last evening came, and the candles were lighted. What a brilliant sight!

"I wonder if the sparrows will come and admire me!" thought the tree. "Will I grow here and be dressed so beautifully all year long? How wonderful that would be!"

Suddenly the parlor doors were thrown open, and the children rushed in. They danced gleefully around the tree, and one present after another was plucked from it. The children rushed about so forcefully that branches cracked and the tree nearly fell down.

"What next?" the fir tree wondered, feeling confused and a little sad.

"Tell us a story!" shouted the children as they drew a little fat man toward the tree. He sat down beneath it and told the story of Klumpey-Dumpey, who had great troubles, yet married the princess and lived happily ever after. The children clapped their hands. The fir tree had never heard such a wonderful story before.

"Surely I will live happily ever after too," it thought. "I will be dressed every evening with candles and toys, nuts and fruit. How jealous the trees in the forest would be if they could see me then!"

The fir tree stood quiet and thoughtful all night, thinking of its bright future.

In the morning the servants came into the parlor.

"Now I will be dressed again!" thought the foolish tree.

But the servants dragged the tree upstairs to the attic and threw it in a dark corner.

"What am I to do here?" thought the tree. "What will happen to me now?"

Days and nights went by and nobody came to the attic. "Perhaps they want to shelter me from the snow until spring comes," the fir tree said. "If only it were not so dark and lonely here—there isn't even a little hare to visit me!"

"Squeak, squeak!" said two little mice as they crept toward the tree. "Hello, old Christmas tree!"

"I'm not old," said the tree indignantly.

"Tell us where you come from," said the mice. They were very curious. "Tell us about the most beautiful spot on earth! Have you been there?"

"I don't know," replied the tree. "But I know the forest, where the sun shines and the birds sing." And the tree told them all about its youth.

"Oh, how happy you must have been!" said the mice.

"Happy?" said the tree thoughtfully. "Yes—I suppose I was quite happy."

The next night the mice came with four other mice. "Tell us another story!" they said.

So the fir tree told of when it had been hung with golden fruit and toys and lighted candles.

"How merry you must have been!" cried the mice. "What a splendid story!"

The next night a great many mice appeared, and even two rats. The fir tree told them the story of Klumpey-Dumpey, who married the princess.

"Tell us another!" said the rats.

"I don't know any other stories," said the fir tree. So the mice and rats left the attic, and the fir tree was alone once again.

"It was nice when the curious little mice listened to me," sighed the fir tree. "But now that, too, is past. I will be so happy when they take me out of this attic!"

At last one morning people came and dragged the old fir tree outside into the garden. Tulips waved in the breeze, and all the trees were covered with pink blossoms.

"Now I shall live!" said the tree, and it tried to spread its branches proudly. But they were all brittle and yellow. The tree lay forlornly in a corner among the weeds. A boy came and tore the gold star from it. Then he jumped on the branches till they broke.

The fir tree looked at the lovely garden and then at itself. It thought of its youth in the forest and of Christmas Eve and of the little mice in the attic.

"I was happy and I never even knew it!" said the old tree. "I always wanted something else. Now it's all past—gone forever!"

Then the servant came and set fire to the tree. It blazed brightly and sighed deeply, thinking of its happy past and how foolish it had been. Each sigh was like a little shot. And then the tree was burned to ashes.

AWAY IN A MANGER
Traditional Carol

Away in a manger, no crib for a bed,
The little Lord Jesus laid down His sweet head.
The stars in the sky looked down where He lay,
The little Lord Jesus, asleep on the hay.

The cattle are lowing, the Baby awakes,
But little Lord Jesus, no crying He makes.
I love Thee, Lord Jesus, look down from the sky,
And stay by my cradle till morning is nigh.

O LITTLE TOWN OF BETHLEHEM
by Phillips Brooks

O little town of Bethlehem,
How still we see thee lie.
Above thy deep and dreamless sleep
The silent stars go by;
Yet in thy dark streets shineth
The everlasting Light;
The hopes and fears of all the years
Are met in thee tonight.

For Christ is born of Mary;
And gathered all above,
While mortals sleep, the angels keep
Their watch of wond'ring love.
O morning stars together
Proclaim the holy birth,
And praises sing to God the King,
And peace to men on earth!

SILENT NIGHT

by Joseph Mohr

Silent night! Holy night!
All is calm, all is bright,
'Round yon virgin Mother and Child.
Holy infant so tender and mild,
Sleep in heavenly peace,
Sleep in heavenly peace!

Silent night! Holy night!
Shepherds quake at the sight,
Glories stream from heaven afar,
Heavenly hosts sing *alleluia;*
Christ, the Savior, is born,
Christ, the Savior, is born!

WE THREE KINGS OF ORIENT ARE

by John Henry Hopkins, Jr.

We three kings of Orient are;
Bearing gifts, we traverse afar,
Field and fountain, moor and mountain,
Following yonder star.

O star of wonder, star of night,
Star with royal beauty bright,
Westward leading still proceeding,
Guide us to Thy perfect light.

Born a King on Bethlehem's plain,
Gold we bring, to crown Him again,
King forever, ceasing never
Over us all to reign.

THE NIGHT BEFORE CHRISTMAS

by Clement C. Moore

'Twas the night before Christmas
When all through the house
Not a creature was stirring, not even a mouse.
The stockings were hung by the chimney with care,
In hopes that St. Nicholas soon would be there.
The children were nestled all snug in their beds,
While visions of sugarplums danced in their heads.
And Mamma in her kerchief and I in my cap
Had just settled down for a long winter's nap.
When out on the lawn there arose such a clatter,
I sprang from my bed to see what was the matter.
Away to the window I flew like a flash,
Tore open the shutters and threw up the sash.
The moon on the breast of the new-fallen snow
Gave a luster of midday to objects below.
When what to my wondering eyes should appear
But a miniature sleigh and eight tiny reindeer,
With a little old driver, so lively and quick,
I knew in a moment it must be St. Nick.
More rapid than eagles his coursers they came,
And he whistled, and shouted, and called them by name:
"Now, Dasher! Now, Dancer! Now, Prancer and Vixen!
On, Comet! On, Cupid! On, Donder and Blitzen!
To the top of the porch, to the top of the wall!
Now, dash away! Dash away! Dash away all!"
As dry leaves that before the wild hurricane fly,
When they meet with an obstacle, mount to the sky,
So up to the housetop the coursers they flew,
With a sleigh full of toys, and St. Nicholas, too.

And then, in a twinkling, I heard on the roof
The prancing and pawing of each little hoof.
As I drew in my head, and was turning around,
Down the chimney St. Nicholas came with a bound.
He was dressed all in fur, from his head to his foot,
And his clothes were all tarnished with ashes and soot.
A bundle of toys he had flung on his back,
And he looked like a peddler just opening his pack.
His eyes how they twinkled! His dimples how merry!
His cheeks were like roses, his nose like a cherry.
His droll little mouth was drawn up like a bow,
And the beard on his chin was as white as the snow.
The stump of a pipe he held tight in his teeth,
And the smoke, it encircled his head like a wreath.
He had a broad face and a little round belly
That shook, when he laughed, like a bowl full of jelly.
He was chubby and plump, a right jolly old elf,
And I laughed when I saw him, in spite of myself.

A wink of his eye and a twist of his head
Soon gave me to know I had nothing to dread.
He spoke not a word, but went straight to his work,
And filled all the stockings, then turned with a jerk,
And laying his finger aside of his nose,
And giving a nod, up the chimney he rose.
He sprang to his sleigh, to his team gave a whistle,
And away they all flew like the down of a thistle.
But I heard him exclaim ere he drove out of sight,
"Happy Christmas to all, and to all a good night."